D0606193

Michael Emberley

WELCOME BACK SUN

Little, Brown and Company   Boston   Toronto   London

DISCARD

The sun never rose today. When I came home from school, it was dark. When I left for school, it was dark. It has been this way for months.

I live in a small village in Norway, wedged deep in a narrow mountain valley. The sun left our village and went behind the mountains in September. It hasn't come back.

Now it is almost March. Outside, the air is cold and still. The winter night has crawled over us. Nature has fallen asleep. It is this way every year. In Norway we call this season the *murketiden*, the murky time.

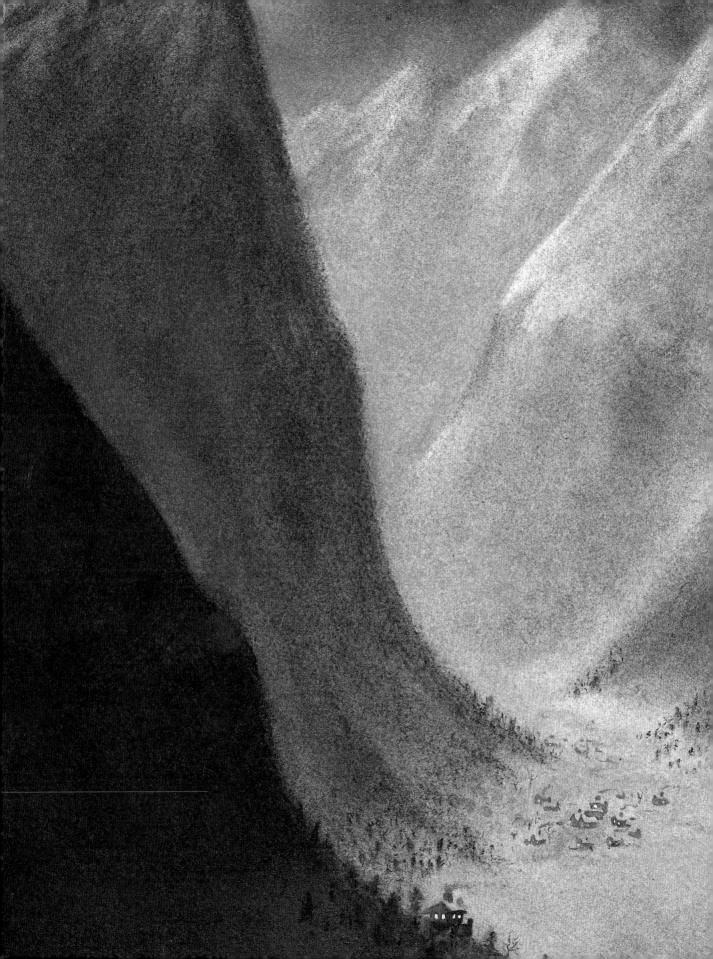

At the beginning of winter, when the sun first disappears, I don't miss it so much. With all the holidays and everyone so busy, I just don't think about it. But after the last Christmas candle is put away, I start to feel the hunger — as if I hadn't eaten for months. By March I am really hungry for sunshine. Papa doesn't seem to feel this hunger, but I know Mama does. It makes her fret and stare and snap at me.

I hate the *murketiden*.

Mama once told me a story of when the sun got lost for the first time, many years ago. After months of darkness in our village, one small girl could not bear it any longer, so she slipped away to search for the sun.

She climbed for days, high into the mountains. The frigid blackness around her screamed with angry Arctic squalls. She struggled through waist-deep snow. She slipped over ice-glazed rocks. On the fourth day, toes nearly frozen, she finally saw a familiar yellow glow coming from behind a tall black crag. She was on the far side of Mount Gausta, the largest of the mountains that wall in our valley, and she had found the lost sun.

With the sun melting a clear path through the snow, the little girl led the way back through the mountains and down to the valley, where the whole village was waiting with hugs, cheers, and warm things to eat.

People today still make the little girl's trek up Mount Gausta to glimpse the sun after a long, dark winter and to show it the way home.

"Could we climb the Gausta, Papa?" I ask one cold, dark morning. "Like the girl in the story?"

"It will be time soon," says Papa, "time for the sun to come back." He gives me a tired smile. Papa works inside all day. He leaves early in the morning and comes home late. He never sees any sunlight during winter. He says that sometimes, it's hard for him even to remember what sunshine looks like.

A week has passed, and the sky brightens
now at noontime. Mama and I go out in the short daylight
to gather budded branches. We will bring the cuttings inside
and place them by a window in water.

"The buds will open there before they do outside," Mama says.
"They will tell us when spring has come." When we are ready to
go home, the brightness is already fading. Quickly we slip over the
snow back to the village, racing the dark. Before I close the door
behind me, I pause and watch the last pale light leave, slowly giving
the sky back to black.

The paper said the sun rose in the south today. In the city of Oslo, the streets were full of dancing people wearing sunny costumes and playing sunny music. It was a holiday. But here in our village, the sun is still hiding. Each day I watch the sky. Each day I examine the branches, fingering each closed bud. But the *murketiden* goes on.

"Couldn't we climb the Gausta?" I ask Mama. "Like the girl in the story?"

"We will wait," says Mama. "The sun will be back soon."

It is now long past the time when the sun came back last year.

"It should be any day now," Papa says.

But bad weather has come into our valley. Thick gray clouds block out all light in the sky, even the brightness. For the first time, I see the strain of the murky time in Papa's eyes. He was stronger than us, but now he, too, craves the sun's warm yellow rays on his face. He, too, hungers for the color and life that the sun gives every-thing it touches.

I climb into Papa's lap. "Couldn't we climb the Gausta?" I ask softly.

Papa looks at Mama. I know at once we will go. Together. It has been a long, dark winter for all of us.

That night, Papa, Mama, and I pack food for the trip: cheese and flat bread, smoked salmon, and some water. From my bedroom window, I see stars. The clouds have slipped away. Tomorrow will be clear.

We get up early. Outside it is cold, but I cannot feel it. A thick crust is on the snow. I walk on top of it, but Papa falls through. Dark shapes crunch up the trail ahead of us. Some carry skis. They need to see the sun, too. They also cannot wait.

The trail, pocked with craters from other climbers' boots, is hard work for everyone. Some will be going all the way to the top of Mount Gausta, but we will go only as far as the pass. It will be high enough.

As we stop to rest, others pass in the half-light, puffing out white clouds. No one climbs past without a smile and a wave. Few will get much work done today. Bosses and teachers will understand. Any Norwegian would.

Now we're hiking faster. The closer we get, the brighter the sky becomes on the crest of the pass. Mama squeezes my hand, hot and sweaty inside my rough wool mitten. My legs hurt, I am breathing hard, but I am not complaining.

"Almost there," whispers Mama. My heart is thumping.

Suddenly the sky explodes with brilliant light. I shield my eyes and squint. The brilliance flashes off snow and ice. It glitters and sparkles off rocks and trees. At last we have reached the pass — and the sun.

Hundreds of people pepper the white ridge, gazing at the splendor of simple sunshine, refreshing memories, and warming spirits. Scattered happy shouts echo on the mountain. Some of us dance. I can't stop smiling.

We eat our salmon, sitting on a black rock warmed by the sun. I close my eyes and face the dimming glow, chewing and smiling, smiling and chewing.

Soon we have to leave. It is already getting colder. As we pack our things, I start yawning. Papa lifts me to his woolly, warm back. I shut my eyes. I don't remember the trip home.

I wake up later in my bed, then thunder downstairs. "The sun followed us," Mama says. "It peeked into the valley and touched the house, while you were sleeping."

We go to the window so I can see the sun on the snow. Then I notice the branches.

There, on a gnarled twig, the first buds have opened. The first tiny splash of colour on an old grey canvas. Spring has finally come.

Welcome back, Sun!

Copyright © 1993 by Michael Emberley

All rights reserved. No part of this book may be reproduced in any form or by
any electronic or mechanical means, including information storage and
retrieval systems, without permission in writing from the publisher, except by a
reviewer who may quote brief passages in a review.

First Edition

Library of Congress Cataloging-in-Publication Data

Emberley, Michael.
 Welcome back, Sun / Michael Emberley.
  p. cm.
 Summary: During *murketiden,* the dark months between September
and March, a Norwegian girl and her family try to hasten the arrival
of spring.
 ISBN 0-316-23647-0
 [1. Sun—Fiction. 2. Spring—Fiction. 3. Norway—Fiction.]
I. Title.
PZ7.E566We   1993
[E]—dc20   92-9786

10 9 8 7 6 5 4 3 2

NIL

Published simultaneously in Canada
by Little, Brown & Company (Canada) Limited

Printed in Italy

JUV
PZ
7
.E566
W4
1993